DYING TO MEET YOU

First published 2008 by
A & C Black Publishers Ltd
38 Soho Square, London, W1D 3HB

www.acblack.com

ISBN: 978-0-7136-8573-2

A CIP catalogue for this book is available from the British Library.

Printed and bound in Great Britain
by CPI Cox & Wyman, Reading RG1 8EX.

DYING TO MEET YOU

Michael Cox
Illustrated by Cathy Brett

A & C Black • London

Chapter One
And the Winners Are...

It was time for the winning entry to be announced and the whole class was positively *bursting* with excitement. Their teacher, Mr Reece, reached deep into the pocket of his green velvet pants, pulled out an envelope, slid a piece of paper from it and took a deep breath.

'Dear Squidgy Buns,' he said. 'Meet me in the bushes behind the science lab. My test tube bubbleth over... Big wet kisses, Cuddly Cakes. Oops! Wrong envelope!' He quickly screwed up the piece of paper, then pulled out another envelope, this time a golden one, from the same pocket.

'Ah, *that's* more like it!' he said, tearing it open and taking out a sparkling silver card. 'And the winners are...'

'Me! Me!' screamed Dwayne Dobson, leaping around like a demented bedbug. 'It's got to be me! I'm the goodest writer in the whole world!'

Mr Reece gave Dwayne the sort of look that people normally reserve for the soles of their shoes when they've just stepped in something unpleasant.

Dwayne winced, then slid beneath his desk and pulled his T-shirt over his head.

'And the winners are...' continued Mr Reece. 'Hailey and Hugo Huckleberry!'

The whole class began clapping wildly as the twins rose to their feet, grinning from ear to ear.

Hailey and Hugo Huckleberry couldn't have been happier! After weeks of high-energy thinking and intensive scribbling, followed by months of nail-biting anticipation, they now knew that the thing they wanted more than anything in the world was finally in their grasp.

Six months ago, along with thousands of other eager young horror-fiction fans, Mr Reece's class of twelve-somethings had entered a nationwide competition to come up with the most imaginative, well-written description of the legendary, best-selling writer of children's horror stories: Chad Piranha.

And that was a very *special* sort of challenge. Why? Because, with the exception of a few close friends and relatives, including Chad's mum (Natasha), Chantelle (his hairdresser) and his dyslexic editor, Tamara Tippex-Tripewrangler, no one had ever seen the famously camera-shy and reclusive author in the flesh. He had never appeared on TV, and his photo had never been in the newspapers. So none of the competition entrants had a clue what Chad Piranha looked like. Which made the whole thing at least 100 times more exciting, challenging and intriguing.

And the prize for all this effort? Well, not only would the winners get to meet the mysterious Chad, they would spend an entire weekend with the great author at his remote hideaway, Macabre Manor, a vast, timbered mansion that nestled in the shadow of the Double Bluff twin peaks, the highest of the wild and lonely Ratskill mountains. In other words, the very place the great writer had penned such masterpieces as *Nightmare At Heaving Bog*, *The Dotty Dog of Doom*, *Melvin's Arm* and, most recently, *Toilet of Terror*.

After much sifting and sorting by the competition judges, the two best entries had been narrowed down to just one class, in one school. Yes – Mr Reece's! And now, Hailey and Hugo Huckleberry knew for sure they would soon be boarding a Queezy Jet 13 and winging their way to Ratskill County. And there, accompanied by the beautiful Tamara Tippex-Tripewrangler, they would finally get to meet their hero.

'I am so, *so* proud of you, Hugo!' beamed Mr Reece, shaking Hailey by the hand.

'You, too, Hailey!' he grinned, patting Hugo on the back.

'I'm Hugo,' said Hugo.

'Well, who's *he* then?' said Mr Reece, indicating Hailey.

'He's Hailey!' said Hugo.

'*Whatever*,' laughed Mr Reece, who, despite having been their teacher for two years, still had problems telling the twins apart. 'The main thing is that you *both* truly, truly deserve to win!'

Then, once again, the class began to applaud their fellow pupils' achievement.

But one person *wasn't* clapping. Nor was he smiling. In fact, as Dwayne Dobson finally crawled out from under his desk, it was plain to see that he was actually 'aglow' with envy, his skin now having turned greener than an environmentalist's cardigan.

But did the class take the slightest bit of notice? Not at all! And they didn't even bat an eyelid when corduroy-clad, stamp-collecting, train-spotting Dwayne snatched the roses from the vase on Mr Reece's desk and ate the lot, washing them down with the yucky green water they'd been standing in for the last six days. In fact, apart from a few comments of 'stupid attention seeker!' they continued applauding the twins.

9

You don't grow up with a kid weirder than a striped dalmatian and get fazed by something as commonplace as him eating a bunch of flowers. In the Dwayne Dobson book of bizarre behaviour, eating flowers would have only rated a 'MAD 1.5' on his weirdometer. Dwayne Dobson was capable of much more unexpected and unsettling acts of complete craziness. Especially if they were fuelled by insane envy, smouldering passion, plus an uncontrollable craving for revenge. As Hailey and Hugo Huckleberry would soon find out…

Chapter Two
Tamara

Two months later, Hailey and Hugo Huckleberry arrived at Ratskill County Airport where Tamara Tippex-Tripewrangler had arranged to meet them.

Fully prepared for their great adventure, both of them looked magnificent in their brand-new, bright-orange parkas, lime-green mittens, deep-crimson balaclavas and luminous-yellow salopettes.

Their flight hadn't been an easy one. Nor was getting on and off the Queezy Jet 13, mainly because of the giant snowshoes that Hailey and Hugo were wearing on the strict orders of their father, Dr Waldo T. Huckleberry Jr, who was convinced Ratskill County was permanently covered with at least two metres of snow.

As it was, when the twins finally did touch down, there was no sign of snow and the thermometer was topping an unseasonably warm 18 degrees. Consequently, their walk across the concourse was not only extremely embarrassing, but also extremely uncomfortable.

When they reached the arrivals lounge, Hailey and Hugo anxiously studied the crowd of meeters and greeters on the opposite side of the barrier, hoping to spot their chaperone-to-be. At the same time, they did their best to ignore the cruel laughter coming from the shorts and T-shirt-wearing bystanders, who stared in disbelief at the oddly dressed new arrivals.

After several checks with the rather out-of-date photograph of a 10-year-old Tamara that Chad's publishers, Dead Good Books, had sent them, Hailey suddenly yelled, 'There she is, Hugo! Well, at least I *think* that's her...'

She was pointing to a tall, blonde woman with lips like ripe tomatoes and teeth like tombstones, who was wearing mirrored sunglasses, a pink angora sweater, purple leather ski-pants and red snakeskin stilettos. A massive fur coat was slung over her shoulders, which trailed behind her like a hairy wedding dress.

The woman was struggling violently with two small, tearful children, and doing her best to drag them towards a pink, open-top roadster, which was parked in the middle of the flowerbed at the airport drop-off point.

'Waaagh!' screamed the children. 'We want our mummy! We want our mummy!'

'I don't get it!' the woman screeched. 'If you don't *want* to meet the greatest children's author on the planet, why did you enter the competition?'

At this point, Hailey spotted the placard that was lying at the woman's feet. On it, were scrawled the words: WELLCOMB - HIGHLY AND HUGELY UGLYBOTTY! and she now knew for certain that this was their escort-to-be.

Grabbing Hugo by the hand, she rushed over to the struggling trio, picked up the placard, held it in front of the woman's face and cried, 'Hi, Tamara. We're Highly and Hugely!'

'Highly and hugely *what*?' snapped Tamara. 'Overdressed? Shy? Sensitive to the cold? Go and annoy someone else, you *freaks*! Can't you see I'm busy.'

'No, no!' said Hailey, pointing to the placard. 'We're the Uglybotties.'

'You're certainly *that*,' said Tamara, glancing at their triple-padded salopettes.

'She means the Huckleberrys,' said Hugo, whipping off first his, then Hailey's, balaclava. 'See! We're the kids who won the "Meet Chad Piranha" competition.'

Tamara's jaw dropped. First she looked at the sobbing kids, then at the twins, then back at the kids, before finally saying, 'So who are *these* two then?'

She never did find out. At that moment,

an extremely angry and anxious-looking couple came rushing up, grabbed the kids and hurried them away.

'Oh, I'm so, *so* sorry, guys!' gasped Tamara, realising her error. 'How can you ever forgive me?'

'It's easily done,' said Hailey. 'We all make mistakes.'

'Yeah, think nothing of it,' said Hugo. 'By the way, you aren't by any chance *short-sighted*, are you?'

'Just a bit,' shrugged Tamara. 'But not so that it's a problem.' Then, glancing at her watch, she cried, 'Hey, guys, it's already a quarter after one! At this rate we won't make Chad's place before dark. And then there's no telling *what* will happen.'

'What do you mean?' asked Hailey.

'Oh, nothing, nothing...' said Tamara, fiddling furiously with a set of lucky charms. 'Everything's going to be fine. Just fine.' And she bustled them out of the arrivals lounge.

As they made their way across the flowerbed to Tamara's pink roadster, chattering excitedly about their forthcoming adventure, a commotion broke out behind them. It began with angry muttering amongst the crowds and quickly swelled to cries of alarm, accompanied by shouts of 'There he is!', 'Don't let him get away!' and 'Hey, you! Stop, or we'll shoot!'. Soon it had grown to a deafening racket, which was almost impossible to ignore.

Seconds later, and quite *terrifyingly*, the air suddenly became filled with the shocking *rat-a-tat-tat* of machine-gun fire, the ear-bending clatter of helicopter rotors, the heart-stopping *thud* of exploding grenades and the hysterical screaming of women and children.

Had the twins and Tamara taken the trouble to look back, they would have most certainly seen the cause of all this pandemonium. Namely, the small, corduroy-clad figure, who was sprinting hell-for-leather along the airport runway, closely followed by a posse of security men, a dozen guard dogs and four police cars.

But they didn't! The twins and their beautiful escort were far, *far* too excited about the prospect of their date with the world's most-famous and celebrated author of children's horror fiction.

So, exchanging a mere shrug as one of the police cars crashed into an incoming Queezy

Jet 13 and a rocket-propelled smoke bomb exploded in the club-class departure lounge, they piled into Tamara's pink roadster and set off for the distant Ratskills. All three of them were blissfully unaware of the rapidly unfolding chain of events which would soon lead to them being caught up in the sort of hair-raising drama that not even a children's horror-fiction writer as talented as Chad Piranha could have dreamed up…

Chapter Three
The High Ratskills

'So!' said Tamara, as the three of them sped along the Ratskill County interstate highway. 'How was the flight from Albania?'

'It was Alabama, actually,' said Hailey.

'Ah, *Alabama*,' said Tamara. 'So *that's* why you guys speak English so good!'

'Anyway, the flight was great,' said Hailey. 'It was our first time.'

'So we were a bit *scared*,' said Hugo, 'but the flight attendant told us it was the safest way to travel. Then we felt OK.'

'Yes, she said it's safer than by car,' added Hailey. 'By the way, Tamara, did you know you're driving on the wrong side of the road?'

'Oh, so I am!' screeched Tamara. 'Shoooot! I am *such* a scatterbrain. You wouldn't believe the amount of wrecks I'm in! Why, only last week I ended up in a 16-car pile-up when I was distracted by a couple of maniacs winding down their windows and yelling at me.'

'That wasn't very nice of them,' said Hailey. 'What were they yelling?'

'Something about how I shouldn't have been texting and eating a bacon sandwich whilst doing 110 on the hard shoulder!' said Tamara. 'Cops! They can be such a *pain*, can't they? Thing is, guys, I'm a speed freak! And this little beauty of mine can do 180, no probs. Here, I'll show you!'

'We'd rather you didn't,' said Hailey.

But Tamara didn't appear to be listening.

In the desperate hope that it might take her mind off cars and speed and stop her killing them before they got to meet their hero, Hailey said, 'Tamara, my brother and I are really looking forward to meeting Chad. What's he like?'

At once, Tamara sighed a huge sigh and went dreamy-eyed. Then, flicking the roadster onto 'cruise control' and dropping her seat to 'maximum recline', she slowed to a steady 50, and whispered, 'Hmmm, well, for starters he's really tall and incredibly handsome. And terribly strong and athletic. Plus he's kind and thoughtful. A real gentleman, too. And lots of fun to be with.'

'We just *knew* he would be!' cried the twins excitedly.

'Yeah, he's very, *very* cool,' said Tamara, with a faraway look in her eyes. 'I often go up to Macabre Manor for the weekend and we go over his writing together. Doing important editing work like checking his nuns, abjectives and the length of his parachutes. Stuff like that.'

'Don't you mean paragraphs?' said Hailey.

'Yes, them,' said Tamara, the distant look still in her eyes. 'We check his suppositories, too. He's very particular about them. He insists that I make sure he's got them placed in just the right spot.'

'*Suppositories!*' spluttered Hugo, looking shocked. 'Aren't they the things people stuff up their b—'

'APOSTROPHES!' cried Hailey, before her brother could finish. 'I think Tamara meant to say *apostrophes!*'

'Yes, those are the ones,' said Tamara. 'I help Chad with them all. Then, when we're done, we sit on the big bearskin rug in front of his log fire, sipping red wine and staring at the flames.'

'What? A *real* bearskin rug with the head and all?' said Hugo, looking impressed.

'It sure is!' said Tamara. 'Chad shot the bear and skinned it with his own hands. He told me how he slit its stomach open with his big hunting knife then pulled out all the gory gizzards and stuff.'

'It sounds *very* romantic,' said Hailey.

'Uuurgh! Get away with you!' exclaimed Tamara. 'How can you think pulling out some dead thing's squidgy bits is romantic?'

'No, not that!' said Hailey. 'I was talking about the sitting by a log fire on a cold evening.'

'Oh, yeah, that's *ever* so romantic!' said Tamara. 'And on *hot* evenings, we sit out on his porch and eat frozen-yoghurt ice cream while we watch the fireflies lighting up the woods.' She paused for a moment, then added, 'Or sometimes it's the arsonist who lights up the woods.'

'ARSONIST?' exclaimed the twins.

'That's right,' said Tamara. 'Just lately, Chad's been having a few problems with some masked nutcase. He lurks in the forest watching Chad's house through binoculars, taking photographs of him when he's hanging out his washing and calling out stuff like, 'You stupid, best-selling author, you! You wear big lady's pants, you do!'

Then, when Chad's least expecting it, this maniac rushes out of the trees and tries to torch his log store, burn down his house, or set his legs on fire when he's not looking.'

'But that's *terrible!*' gasped the twins.

Tamara shrugged and said, 'You get some odd types up here in the hills. Fugitives on the run from the law. Kidnappers. Escaped murderers. All kinds.'

Then, seeing the children's terrified expressions, she quickly added, 'But don't be scared, guys. You've got me and Chad to look after you.'

The sky had now turned the colour of a hanged-man's tongue and a vicious north-east wind was howling like a banshee as it whipped ragged, yellowish-purple clouds across the distant mountain tops.

'Looks like snow!' said Tamara, gazing upwards.

'What does?' said the twins, their minds still full of arsonists, murderers and big lady's pants.

'Frozen-yoghurt ice cream,' said Tamara.

'Yup,' said the twins. 'Guess it does, now you come to mention it.'

They'd turned off the busy interstate highway some time ago and were now climbing the long and lonely road that would eventually take them to the wildest and remotest parts of the High Ratskills and eventually to Chad's hideaway. They started to leave behind all signs of human habitation and, as Tamara's roadster ascended a steep mountain pass, negotiating one terrifying hairpin bend after another, they entered a landscape of awesome, snow-covered peaks, sheer drops, deep gorges, tumbling rivers and gloomy forests. They also began to pass signs to scary-sounding places like Skeleton Lake, Murder Canyon, Poisoner's River and, most alarming of all, Massacre Ridge.

Two hours later, with snowflakes swirling around Tamara's roadster, the wind moaning in the trees and the timber wolves whining on distant ridges, the twins suddenly spotted a little sign which said: Double Bluff - 3 miles.

'Almost there!' said Tamara. 'Pity I can't call Chad on my mobile and tell him to warm up some muffins and put the kettle on. The coverage in these parts is hopeless!'

'I can't believe we're gonna be at his place any time now!' said the excited twins.

'Too right!' cried Tamara. 'In just a few short moments we'll all be sitting in front of his big log fire having the time of our lives.'

How wrong she would turn out to be. As they rounded the next bend, the weary travellers saw something that made their hearts leap and their pulses race. Lying in the road a short distance ahead of them was a large and extremely sinister-looking object. However, what with the gathering gloom and the increasingly frequent snow flurries, it was hard to make out exactly what it was. But, as they drew nearer, Tamara suddenly screamed, 'Oh, my good *Gob*! It's a *man*!'

Chapter Four
The Mutant

'Are you sure?' said the twins.

'Yes!' cried Tamara, bringing the roadster to a skidding halt. 'I'm sure of it. It's a really, really big man!' She quickly reached for her handbag, took out her cosmetics case and began frantically redoing her lipstick and fluffing her hair. Then she turned to the twins, flashed them a dazzling smile and squealed, 'Well... how do I look?'

'Er... very, er... nice,' said Hailey.

'Yes, er... smashing,' said Hugo.

'Check,' said Tamara. 'Now, I think it's time I had a word with that... man!' Bent almost double against what was now turning into an all-out blizzard, she climbed out of her car and began to battle her way towards the large, and (somewhat worryingly) contorted and immobile figure which lay in their path.

'I wonder what he's doing?' said Hailey.

'Maybe he felt tired,' said Hugo. 'And decided to have a little rest?'

'Don't be *silly*, Hugo,' snapped Hailey. 'Apart from Chad's place, we're 100 miles from the nearest human habitation, and it's snowing. Of course he's not *having a rest*!'

'Yes, I suppose you're right,' said Hugo. 'So what do you think he *is* doing, sis?'

'It's perfectly obvious,' said Hailey. 'Well, it is to anyone with a crumb of intelligence. He's making some sort of eco-protest. You know, like "Save the Trees" or "Don't Make Any More Holes in the Ozone Layer".'

'Of course,' said Hugo, as Tamara neared the vertical figure. 'He's managing to stay very *still*, isn't he?'

'Yes, he is,' agreed Hailey. 'And he also seems to have more than the usual amount of arms and legs.'

'Hmm, so he does,' said Hugo. Then, as a horrible and totally unwelcome thought entered his head, he let out a gasp of terror and moaned, 'Oh dear, I hope he's not some sort of escaped, multi-limbed, laboratory experiment that's gone wrong…'

'Who is now on the rampage in search of

fresh human flesh…' added Hailey, her 'twin-telepathy' enabling her to scramble aboard her brother's terrifying train of thought. 'And pretending to be hurt in order to lure the pretty young children's fiction editor into a trap which will most certainly end in her painful *demise*!'

'Or even,' gasped Hugo, turning whiter than the snow that had now completely coated their lovely young chaperone, 'her agonising *death*!'

The hairs on the back of the twins' necks stood on end.

'TAMARA!' screamed Hailey. 'Don't take another step. You are in terrible, terrible danger. What you see before you is not a simple eco-warrior protesting against global warming, but a multi-limbed mutant…'

'Who has recently escaped from a lavatory…' added Hugo.

'And is after your *flesh*!'

'In other words,' concluded Hugo, 'he's more of a *mentalist* than an environ-*mentalist*!'

But it was too late.

Tamara was already kneeling beside the figure, gesturing frantically in the direction of her car in what was obviously a heartfelt request to let them pass.

'Oh, poor Tamara!' screamed Hailey. 'At any moment that freak is going to tear her limb from limb, then sink his fangs into her.'

Chapter Five
D - U - D!

Hailey covered her eyes and sobbed. 'Oh, it's too, *too* horrible! I simply can't look!'

'It's OK, sis!' said Hugo. 'I'll describe it all for you as it happens.'

'So,' whimpered Hailey, a few agonising moments later. 'Is poor Tamara being torn to shreds by the monstrous laboratory-experiment-gone-wrong?'

'No,' said Hugo.

'What's happening then?' said Hailey.

'She's beating him up,' said Hugo.

'She's *what?*' gasped Hailey, removing her hands from her eyes to see that, yes, Tamara *was* now energetically pummeling the stricken figure.

'Oh, Hugo, you numbskull!' she cried. 'Tamara's not beating him up. She's giving the poor man *resuscitation*. He's probably half-frozen to death. And here's us thinking he was some sort of mutant cannibal. We must go and help!'

A moment later, the blizzard raging around them, the twins were crouched next to the breathless Tamara.

'He's not responding,' she gasped. 'I think he may be…' She paused, put her hand over her mouth, then slowly whispered, 'D – U – D!'

'Dud?' said Hugo. 'What's *dud*?'

'I think she means *dead*,' said Hailey.

'Yes, that's it!' said Tamara. 'I think he's dud! I've tried giving him cardy-and-pullover restoration, but it's no use. Now I think Roger Mortis must be setting in. See how his limbs are sticking out, all stiff and lifeless.'

'That's because he's a tree,' said Hugo.

'A tree?' said Tamara.

'Yes, Tamara,' said Hailey. 'He's a tree. If you look really carefully, you'll see that he's got branches and a trunk and twigs and stuff.'

'Hmmm, yes, I see what you mean,' said Tamara, peering closely at her patient. 'I thought his skin was a bit wrinkled and coarse to the touch.'

'She really is short-sighted, isn't she?' whispered Hailey.

'And I don't think those mirrored sunglasses help, either,' muttered Hugo. 'Especially now they're completely covered with ice.'

Tamara got to her feet, brushed the snow from her coat, then said, 'But… but… how do you think a tree came to be here?'

'Oh, you know, the usual way,' said Hugo. 'Hundreds of years ago, a passing bird, possibly a penguin, would have dropped a seed. Then, with the help of sunlight and moisture…'

'No, I don't mean *that*!' cried Tamara. 'What I mean is, how do you think it came to be lying across the road? Surely it can't have *grown* that way!'

'No,' said Hailey, suddenly spotting a small heap of wood chips. 'See – it's been cut down!'

'And recently,' added Hugo. 'Look – there's a little pool of fresh sap here in the road. It's still warm.'

'But who would do such a thing?' said Tamara. 'And why?'

'I know,' said Hugo. '*Beavers*!'

'But I thought beavers only cut down the trees by rivers,' said Tamara.

'Well,' said Hailey. 'Maybe *these* beavers were carrying *this* tree to a river. But then, with it

31

being so big and heavy, they became tired.'

'And decided to leave it in the road and come back for it later,' continued Hugo.

'Yes, that would be it,' agreed Hailey.

'Well,' said Tamara, '*we've* got a date with a best-selling author, and we certainly don't have time to wait around for a bunch of beavers to finish their afternoon nap.'

'There's only one thing for it,' said Hugo. '*We'll* have to move it.'

But it was no good. Try as they might, the three of them just couldn't budge the huge tree. It must have weighed at least a ton.

'*Now* what are we going to do?' sighed Hailey, her lower lip quivering fearfully. 'It will be dark in an hour, and this snow is getting worse! Oh dear, I hope this isn't all going to turn into the kind of horror story Chad writes.'

'But without the happy ending,' said Hugo.

'Oh dear!' cried Tamara, completely at a loss. 'I've gone and got us all into a right pickle, haven't I? I'm so useless. First of all I try and pick up the wrong kids. Then I nearly kill us on the highway. And now *this*!'

'Don't worry, Tamara,' said Hailey. 'We all have our bad days.'

But Tamara wasn't to be comforted. 'I'm hopeless!' she wailed. 'Sometimes I even wonder if I'm really up to editing the works of a great writer like Mr Piranha. I mean, who else would mistake a tree for a great big man?'

'It's easily done,' said Hailey. 'Especially if your eyes don't work so good.'

'It's all the reading,' sobbed Tamara. 'It's worn them out.'

All at once, she appeared to make a big decision and with a cry of 'Enough is enough, I'm going to get help!', she ran off into the woods.

'You're wasting your time,' Hugo called after her. 'There's probably not a decent optician within 100 miles of here!'

'Not *that* sort of help,' called Tamara from a rocky, tree-covered slope. 'I mean help to move the really big tree. I'm going to try and get to Chad's place. It's only a couple of miles up the mountain, if you go cross-country.'

'But what about us?' called Hailey.

'No sense in all three of us risking life and limb,' yelled Tamara. 'This forest is teeming with dangerous wild beasts. Grizzly bears. Mountain lions. Wolves. Coyotes. And guinea pigs, too... I think.'

'Uuurgh, guinea pigs,' shivered Hugo. 'I *hate* guinea pigs.'

'Get back in the car,' called Tamara. 'I'll lock the doors with the remote. You'll be perfectly safe.'

'But what about you?' said Hailey.

'Yes!' said Hugo. 'What about the arsonist and the escaped murderers? Aren't you putting yourself in terrible danger?'

'Don't worry about me,' Tamara called bravely. 'I know these woods like the back of my head.'

The twins quickly got back in the roadster and a moment later there was a loud clunk as Tamara clicked the remote, locking all four doors. Then she charged off into the forest.

Their chaperone now gone, the twins exchanged anxious looks.

'It's pretty dark and spooky here, isn't it?' said Hugo.

'Well, I don't know about *pretty*,' said Hailey, 'but it's certainly dark and spooky.'

'And freezing, too,' shivered Hugo. 'Do you think Tamara would mind if we put the roof up?'

'I'm sure she wouldn't,' said Hailey. 'Do you know which button to press?'

'This one, I think,' said Hugo. 'Oh, I love this song!'

'Idiot,' said Hailey. 'Let's try this one.'

'Bingo!' cried Hugo, as the roof slid smoothly into place.

'Hugo,' said Hailey, 'there's a time and a place for everything, and I think the middle of the forest, in circumstances that are both scary and possibly life-threatening is hardly the time to start playing trivial games involving numbers, random possibility and lots of shouting!'

'No, I mean bingo, we've done it!' said Hugo. 'Now all we have to do is sit tight until Tamara gets back with Chad, then everything will be fine.'

But he had hardly finished speaking when the freezing forest air was pierced by a blood-curdling, marrow-chilling scream. It was followed by a second, then a third, each one more blood-curdling and spine-tingling than the last.

Chapter Six
Pleeeeeeease, Help Me!

'What was that?' said Hugo.

'I'm n- n- not sure!' stammered Hailey.

Before either of them could utter another word, three even more blood-curdling screams rang out, this time accompanied by horrid gurgling noises and closely followed by a muffled cry, which sounded very much like someone yelling, 'Help me! PLEEEEEEEASE, HELP ME!' However, as the twins were now screaming at the tops of *their* voices and making their own horrid gurgling noises, it was hard to tell.

Then, just as quickly as they'd begun, the screams stopped and all that could be heard was the rhythmic *splatt*! *splatt*! *splatt*! of snowflakes hitting tree branches and the eerie *too-wit-too-woo*, *too-wit-too-woo* of a nutty squirrel.

Hugo was the first to speak. 'It was probably nothing,' he said with a shrug. 'Just the sound of the wind in the tree tops.'

'Or a forest animal making itself comfortable in its nest,' said his sister.

'Yeah, a guinea pig, or something like that,' said Hugo.

But hardly had he finished speaking when a new noise caused a tidal wave of worry to wash over them. Beginning quietly, but becoming increasingly loud and terrifying, mad laughter began to echo around the gloomy forest. And it was coming from the very spot where they'd last seen Tamara!

Soon this laughter became so *pants-wettingly scary*, Hugo could stand it no longer. Without the slightest thought for his delicate inner organs, he jammed his fists into his ears, shut his eyes and began making *waaah*! *waaah*! noises, whilst occasionally yelling, 'This is not really happening! Ha ha! I can't see it and I can't hear it, so it's not real!'

Hugo's nose started to twitch as an unmistakable smell began to drift up his nostrils. It was the smell of fear. Raw, *nightmare-strength* fear. And, just like a shipload of lunatics that has been washed up on the rocks, Hugo was instantly transformed into a… *gibbering wreck*!

Then, as abruptly as the screams had done, the laughter stopped and a deathly hush fell over the forest once more, broken only by the grunt of a sleeping guinea pig.

'Tamara's taking her time,' said Hailey. 'I wonder what can be slaying her. Sorry, I mean *delaying* her…'

But Hugo, his fists permanently wedged inside his ears and his brains turned to the texture of warm pig-swill, could only grunt and gibber as his sister anxiously surveyed the threatening forest.

Just when it felt like all hope had disappeared and these twenty-first-century babes in the wood were facing a brief and painful future, a huge smile suddenly lit up Hailey's lovely young face. She had spied a movement in the trees.

'Oh, thank goodness!' she exclaimed. 'Look, Hugo, it's Tamara. She's come back!'

'Yes, yes!' cried Hugo. 'And she's grown a *beard*!'

Of course it wasn't Tamara who was making her way towards the twins. It was a tall, powerfully built man, dressed in a deerstalker hat and so many different sorts of animal skins that it looked like he'd recently slaughtered an entire zoo in order to provide himself with a warm, winter outfit.

In his enormous right fist he held an axe. Its shaft was scarred with what may well have been human bite marks, while its blade was wet with something that may have been tree sap, but could equally have been fresh human blood. It was hard to tell in the swirling snow. In his left hand, the man held a gigantic burning torch, while over his shoulder was slung a thick coil of rope.

'Hugo!' said Hailey, as the man came closer. 'Why are you sitting on my knee?'

But Hugo couldn't hear her. He still had his hands firmly jammed inside his ears and was making the *waaah!* *waaah!* noises again. However, after a few moments he stopped *waaah*ing, took one look at the man's enormous, flaming torch and began shouting, 'ARS- ARS- ARS!'

'Arse?' said Hailey, puzzled. 'Hugo, *read my lips*. Are you trying to tell me something about the big man's *bottom*?'

Hugo shook his head frantically then looked at his own trousers and yelled, 'ARS- ARS!'

'Oh,' said Hailey. 'You're trying to tell me something about *your* bottom!'

Hugo shook his head again and began making crackling and spitting noises that made him sound a bit like a roaring fire.

'Ah, got you!' cried Hailey. 'You mean *arsonist*. You think the man with the big flaming torch is the arsonist Tamara was telling us about.'

Hugo opened his eyes as wide as they would go, then nodded his head so frantically that Hailey began to worry that it might actually fall off.

'And you think he wants to set your trousers on fire?' said Hailey.

Hugo nodded even more frantically.

'And you don't *want* him to set your trousers on fire, do you?'

Hugo shook his head again and began to cry.

'Stop that this minute, Hugo!' said Hailey. 'As long as we're inside the car we won't come to any harm. Don't forget, Tamara's locked us in. So there's absolutely nothing to worry about. We're completely safe from the big man with the axe.'

There was a loud clunk as the latches on all four of the roadster's doors sprang open. Then the doors *themselves* sprang open. Hailey looked at the man. He was grinning like a maniac and pointing to the silver object that he clutched in his other hand.

It was Tamara's car key.

Chapter Seven
Chad Piranha

Hailey grabbed the handle of the door nearest her and slammed it shut. But then there was a buzzing noise and the electric window slid down, once more leaving the twins terrifyingly exposed to the mad axeman.

Hugo started to cry again, even louder. Hayley looked at the enormous, hairy hand which had now appeared next to her own small, trembling one and at the huge, moustachioed face which was filling the space formerly occupied by the car window.

'Hi!' said a voice as warm and reassuring as freshly baked apple pie and custard. 'You must be Hailey. Thought I might find you here. Piranha's the name, *Chad* Piranha. I think it's time we got you guys somewhere safe and warm.'

When she heard the words she had started to think she would never hear, Hailey burst into tears. But, unlike her twin brother's, they were tears of relief. She was so overwhelmed that this man wasn't the arsonist or an escaped murderer, she was unable to say a single word. At the same time, she was filled with awe at finally being in the presence of her hero.

Eventually, she found her voice and whispered, 'Oh, Mr Piranha, thank you. Thank you for coming to rescue us. I think you may have arrived in the nick of time.'

'All part of the service,' the big man laughed. 'And *please*, call me *Chad*!' Then he looked at Hugo and said, 'And I guess this must be Hugo.'

'Yes, it is,' said Hailey. 'I'm afraid he's got his hands jammed in his ears.'

'So I see,' said Chad. 'Does he do it often?'

'All the time,' giggled Hailey. 'He loves it. And sometimes he stuffs them under his armpits, or up his nostrils.' Then she added quickly, 'No, not really, I just made that up. He only does it when he's frightened.'

'Well, there's certainly nothing to be scared of now,' said Chad. 'As soon as we get to my house, we'll see what we can do about getting him unstuck. Some warm olive oil and a size 16 monkey wrench should have them out in a jiffy!' He patted Hugo on the head, and Hugo grinned up at him like a battery chicken that's just been told it's being sent to live with a vegetarian.

Chad now turned his attention to the big tree and said, 'But first we must get rid of that, or we won't be going anywhere. You two sit tight and I'll have it sorted in a flash. I used to work at a logging company. I was senior *branch* manager!' Then he laughed loudly.

Hailey remembered how Tamara had said what fun Chad was to be with. She certainly hadn't been exaggerating. Nor was she exaggerating when she'd described Chad as being incredibly strong and athletic. As the twins watched, the axe was no more than a blur of movement in his huge hands. In just three minutes he'd done the impossible, and reduced the entire tree to neatly stacked log piles.

'OK, guys!' he cried, nimbly vaulting into the driving seat of the soft top. 'Let's go eat some muffins!' And, with that, he turned the key in the ignition, slammed the roadster into gear and roared off up the hill, scattering logs as he went.

'Er, Chad,' said Hailey, 'I think you've forgotten your flaming torch!'

Chad gave Hailey a shocked look, 'I say, there's no need for *that* sort of language, young lady.' Then he elbowed her in the ribs and said, 'Only joking!' and Hailey realised that she and brother were in for a weekend of japes, jokes… and lots of bruises.

As Chad drove, humming happily to himself, spinning the steering wheel with the confidence of a grand-prix racer and taking corners at breakneck speed, Hailey couldn't help staring at his ruggedly handsome features and thinking how lucky she and Hugo were. She was truly in awe of him. In fact, she was so in awe that she decided not to mention the huge hole he'd made in the canvas roof of Tamara's roadster when he vaulted into the driving seat. So, instead of mentioning that, she asked him where Tamara was.

Chad passed a hand across his magnificent jaw of freshly trimmed designer stubble and said, 'Ah, Tamara... well, she didn't actually make it *back* to my place.'

Chapter Eight
Macabre Manor

'She *didn't*?' said Hailey, a small jolt of fear clutching her heart.

'Well, not right away, she didn't. But she's there now. So there's nothing to worry about,' said Chad, sensing her concern. 'I was gathering firewood when I came across her in the woods. And seeing how cold and distressed she was, I sent her on to my place with instructions to warm up a storm of muffins and put the kettle on.' Then he laughed heartily and cried, 'Though I think she's gonna look a bit stupid wearing a kettle!' And the twins laughed, too.

Feeling slightly more relaxed now, Hailey decided to mention something that had been bothering her for a while. 'Chad,' she said, 'some time between Tamara setting off and you arriving to rescue us, Hugo and I heard the most terrible screams coming from the direction that Tamara had taken. To be honest, it sounded like she was in some sort of trouble. But then the screams stopped and after that we heard mad laughter echoing around the forest. It gave us both a real fright.'

'Oh that,' laughed Chad. 'Yes, I suppose it might have sounded scary to someone not "in-the-know". Thing is, when I found Tamara she was having a confrontation with a very large noose. Sorry, I mean *moose*. It had her pinned up against a tree and she was screaming fit to bust. But, just as I was about to see it off, she punched it on the nose – *bop!* Just like that. The moose was so shocked, it took off into the woods with Tamara tearing after it, shaking her fist and calling it every name under the sun. It was the funniest thing I've seen in years. That laughter you heard was me splitting my sides.'

'Oh, well that's all right,' said Hailey. Then she remembered something else and said, 'By the way, Chad, I think you may have left your rope in the woods, too.'

But Chad wasn't listening. He was pointing a tiny remote control at a huge metal gate with a sign on it that read: KEEP OUT! TRESPASSERS WILL BE GIVEN A GOOD TALKING TO.

The massive gate slowly slid aside to reveal an enormous timber-clad mansion surrounded by immaculate lawns, elegant shrubberies and huge flowerbeds full of sleeping flowers.

'OK, guys, here we are,' said Chad 'My *humble* little backwoods shack.'

Of course, he was joking again. Chad's fabulous mansion was all the twins had expected and more. In fact, it was positively brilliant!

Parked outside was a huge Bully Boy 'Squirrel Squidger' 4x4 with a golden 'CHAD PARANOIA' personalised number plate (Chad hadn't been able to find a 'PIRANHA' one so he'd had to settle for the nearest thing). And next to that was a whole fleet of other luxury vehicles.

Just past the drive stood a warmly lit stable block where it was possible to see six or seven magnificent polo ponies contentedly chewing hay, neighing companionably to each other and doing all the other stuff that top-of the-range-horses do. Beyond the stables were tennis courts, an Olympic-size swimming pool, a miniature railway, a go-kart circuit, a ten-pin bowling alley and a helicopter pad with a bright-orange WhirlyBird 123GO! helicopter parked on it.

'WOW!' gasped Hugo, his fists still firmly jammed in his ears. 'IT'S ABSOLUTELY AWESOME!'

'Are we in for some fun?' said Hailey.

'I don't know,' smiled Chad. 'You tell me!'

Hailey laughed, then said, 'It's a wonder you find time to write all your amazing books!'

'I *work* hard and I *play* hard!' said Chad, then he bounded up the front steps of his mansion, flung open the door and ushered the children into a vast hall filled with antiques, classical sculptures, fabulous oil paintings and the complete set of Pokemon characters from 1995 to 2004.

'Welcome to Macabre Manor,' said Chad, taking off his deerstalker and sending it spinning across the hall. It landed on the head of a stuffed grizzly bear, which stood at the bottom of an ornate oak staircase. 'Tamara!' he bellowed. 'We're home!'

But there was no reply.

Chapter Nine
Tamara Never Comes

'TAMARA! WE'RE BACK!' yelled Chad. 'COME AND SAY HI TO THE KIDS!'

But there was still no reply.

Hailey and Hugo exchanged worried glances.

'Do you think she's... she's... OK?' said Hailey.

'Of course she is,' laughed Chad, with a brief shrug. 'This place of mine is so huge, she could be anywhere. In the home cinema! Ice skating! At the fun fair riding the ferret wheel...'

'Don't you mean *ferris* wheel?' said Hailey.

'No,' said Chad. 'It's a ferret wheel. You know, just like a hamster wheel, except it's powered by hundreds of scampering ferrets.

'Now, where was I? Yes, Tamara! She could also be in my huge kitchen busily rustling us up a huge beef casserole for dinner. Or maybe she's decided to curry the polo ponies instead.'

At this, Hailey went weak at the knees.

The twins had heard that Chad had a few odd tastes and habits. After all, he *was* an author. But the thought of having to eat polo-pony tikka-masala was asking *too* much, even of them.

'Chad, do you really think it's right to turn horses into exotic, far-eastern dishes liberally seasoned with herbs and spices?' she said, as politely as she could.

'Ha ha ha!' laughed Chad. 'No, no, no! I didn't mean curry the ponies as in cook them. I meant that perhaps Tamara's gone to *groom* them. You know... with a curry comb.'

'Oh, I get you!' said Hailey. Then she looked thoughtful and added, 'But even so, Tamara still seems to be taking her time. I thought she'd be keen to make sure me and Hugo are OK.'

'Well, you know what they say,' quipped Chad. '*Tamara never comes*! Ha ha ha!'

Which Hailey thought was in rather bad taste, but Hugo laughed loudly, as he still had his fists stuck in his ears and sensed that laughter was required.

Then Chad said, 'Tell you what, kids! While we're waiting for Tamara to turn up, I'll give you a guided tour of the Chad Pad. But first, let's get Hugo's fists out of his ears.'

And, just as Chad had predicted, the warm olive oil worked a treat – Hugo's fists came out of his ears with a resounding pop!

'THANKS, MR PIRANHA! THAT'S LOADS BETTER!' yelled Hugo.

Chad took the twins from room to room, proudly showing them his eight bathrooms, each with its own jacuzzi and walk-in toilet, his fifteen bedrooms, his indoor swimming pool, his private art gallery and library, and lots, lots more. It took over an hour, as he proudly showed them every room in his huge house, all except his massive walk-in freezer, which Chad said wasn't very interesting.

'But you're welcome to go there, if you ever feel like "chilling out",' he joked.

Of course, there was one room the twins wanted to see most...

'Chad, show us where you write your brilliant books!' they cried excitedly.

'My pleasure!' said Chad.

Chad's Scribblarium, as he liked to call it, was packed with hi-tech gadgets of every kind and it wasn't long before he was posing next to his paper shredder, pretending to write at his PC, thoughtfully sharpening his pencils with his collection of novelty pencil sharpeners and making pretend phone calls as the twins snapped away with their new digital cameras. Finally, all three of them posed for a very special shot with Chad's much-prized Children's Horror Writer of the Century 'Golden Entrails' Award.

The tour now over, a small and rather perplexing can't-quite-put-my-finger-on-it thought niggled away at Hailey's brain as Chad shepherded the twins into his sitting room, where a roaring fire blazed in a fireplace big enough to park a donkey in, while a litter of golden-brown muffins purred contentedly in a basket by the hearth.

'Well, that *was* fun,' said Chad, slumping into his rocking chair.

'It certainly was,' sighed Hailey.

'Amazing!' agreed Hugo.

But then they all remembered that Tamara still hadn't turned up.

'This really is so unlike her,' said Chad.

'You… you… don't think that… something horrid might have happened to her, do you?' mumbled Hailey, hardly daring to let the words pass her lips. 'You know, like being kidnapped by an escaped murderer. Or a masked ars… ars… ars…'

'A masked *arse*?' said Chad. 'I hardly think *that's* likely.'

'I was going to say masked arsonist,' said Hailey, now making up her mind to tell Chad how Tamara had told them about the mysterious fire bug. But then she saw the look of terror on Chad's face and thought better of it.

The great writer turned to the big mirror over the fireplace and began anxiously stroking his designer stubble, saying, 'It's no good. It'll be pitch black in an hour and then I won't be able to do a thing. I'm gonna have to phone the cops.'

'They won't be able to help,' said Hailey. 'What you need is a really good safety razor.'

'And some top-of-the-range shaving gel,' added Hugo.

'No, kids,' gasped Chad snatching up his cordless, touch-tone, hands-free viddy phone. 'I'm not talking about my *beard*. I'm gonna call the cops about *Tamara*.' And with that, he rushed out of the room tapping frantically at his handset.

Moments later he came back, ashen-faced and trembling, for now things really *had* taken a turn for the worse!

'The phone lines are down... or cut... or something!' he gasped, his rugged features suddenly contorted by a look of pure terror. 'It's just as I feared. *He's* back!' Then he began gnawing his viddy phone and sobbing violently.

'Chad,' they said. 'What is it?'

'It's a viddy phone,' said Chad. 'This one's got a five-million-pixel image with instant replay.'

'No, Chad,' said Hugo. 'Why are you so upset?'

'Yes,' said Hailey. 'And who's... *he*?' Though she hardly needed to ask. Thoughts of masked arsonists and escaped murderers were ringing deafening alarm bells in her head.

'Yes,' said Hugo. 'Tell us what you mean, Chad. Please, please tell us!'

At these words, Chad pulled himself together. He carefully wiped an enormous cluster of bogeys from the tip of his giant moustache, then gently took Hailey and Hugo's hands in his. 'Look, guys,' he snuffled, 'I'm afraid I've got some bad news for you. We're in really big trouble. Really *very* big trouble. Sort of very big awful *really bad* trouble, actually!'

'What is it?' gasped the twins.

'It's like when bad things happen to you,' said Chad. 'You know, when stuff goes wrong.'

'We know *that*,' said Hailey. 'Just tell us what the problem is!'

'All right... I suppose you'll have to know sooner or later,' the great writer sighed, flopping into his rocking chair. 'Though the last thing I want to do is take the shine off this special weekend of yours. But the truth is there's a 99.9999 per cent chance that all three of us are going die during the next 24 hours. And what's more, we'll probably perish in the most horrible and painful way you can imagine.'

Chapter Ten
Absolute Carp

'No, no, no!' screamed Hailey and Hugo falling to the floor and sobbing pitifully. 'It's not fair! We're too young to die!'

'Hmm,' murmured Chad. 'I had a feeling you might be a bit disappointed.'

'D- d- does this mean we're going to miss our pre-brunch, creative power-skipping session?' stammered Hailey.

'Yes, I'm afraid it does, Hailey,' continued Chad. 'And I don't want to be a wet blanket or anything, but I think we must all prepare for the worst. More likely than not we're going to die by strangulation or frenzied hacking with a semi-sharp instrument, such as a rusty meat cleaver. Anyone fancy a muffin?'

'No thanks, Chad, not right at this moment,' said Hugo.

'What's going on?' whispered Hailey, barely able to speak.

'I'm offering you a muffin,' said Chad.

'WE DON'T WANT ONE, CHAD!' cried Hugo. 'WE WANT TO KNOW WHY WE'RE GOING TO DIE!'

'It's a long story,' said Chad, absent-mindedly picking at his fingernails with a miniature pirate's cutlass from his collection of novelty pencil sharpeners.

'Well, tell it to us!' said Hailey. 'After all, you *are* a master storyteller, aren't you?'

'Hmm, yes… so I am!' said Chad, a warm glow of pride briefly causing his pale face to glow like someone's bottom which has been left out in the sun for too long. 'All right, I will. If you're sitting uncomfortably… I'll begin.'

He trimmed a hangnail from his finger then cleared his throat. 'It's not easy being a famous writer. It's a demanding and stressful job. For starters, there's pencils to sharpen and erasers to replace. Not to mention important decisions to make about which sort of letter font to use and the right height to have my chair at. And there's the fan mail to deal with, too. The stuff from the weirdos is the worst.

'About three years ago, a guy called Sherwood U. Harm wrote, telling me how much he admired my work. At first, his letters were full of the usual stuff that extremely talented and wonderful people like me get all the time. That was fine, I'm a modest sort of guy. I can cope with any amount of flattery and I don't let it go to my head. But then things started to get unpleasant.'

'Why, Chad?' said Hugo.

'He began sending me little samples of his... personal stuff.'

'Urrgh!' said Hugo. 'Stuff like spit and earwax and bogeys and whatnot? That's *disgusting!*'

'No, not that kind of personal stuff,' said Chad. 'He sent me his *writing*! He asked me what I thought of it and for help with getting it published. Well, I'm a busy man, so I sent it to Tamara to look at. And she wrote back saying it was the biggest load of carp she'd ever read.'

'Carp?' said Hailey.

'Yes, absolute carp,' said Chad. 'And when I told him it was carp, his letters started to take on a slightly less friendly tone. Nothing too obvious… just subtle hints of possible unpleasantness that might happen at some point in the future.'

'What like, Chad?' said Hugo.

'You know, stuff like "I'm gonna come up there and suck out your eyeballs then play ping-pong with them, hack off your arms and feed them to the hogs", that sort of thing,' said Chad. 'I got the feeling that he was a bit annoyed with me. And quite soon after that the letters started to get really threatening and *extremely* unpleasant. I began to dread opening my fan mail. And then, just when I thought things couldn't get any worse, the guy turned up in my kitchen.'

'What… just walked in?' exclaimed Hailey.

'No, the mailman brought him,' said Chad. 'He posted himself to me from New Deli.'

'Wow! All the way from India!' exclaimed Hailey.

'No, New Deli Delights of North Dakota,' said Chad. 'I order a hamper full of tasty treats from their Creative Gourmet department every month. I was just in the middle of unpacking a carton of "Seafood Surfari" when he burst out of his jiffy bag and went for me with a crab claw. I grabbed a couple of king prawns and all hell broke loose. I was no match for him, though. He had the strength of ten men; these maniacs always do, you know. He soon had the upper hand and, before I knew it, I was covered from head to toe with Thousand Island dressing and sinking fast. Just when I thought my end had come, a dozen cops burst into the kitchen and rescued me. Seems that Harm's probation officer had broken into his apartment earlier that morning and found a death list hidden inside his dog. And guess who was top of the chops?'

'You, Chad!'

'Got it in one,' shrugged Chad. 'Well, the outcome was that he got three years role-playing therapy at the Wisconsin School of

Corrective Drama Therapy and a guest spot on *The Ten Authors I'd Most Like To Whack*. And I got a big urge to move house and live the quiet life. Which is why I came up here to the Ratskills.'

'To stay out of Harm's way!' said Hailey.

'Exactly! But now he's out… and he's *back*. I suspected as much when Tamara and I spotted the masked arsonist lurking in the woods. And setting stuff on fire isn't the only thing he's been doing! Sherwood U. Harm's also a master of all things technical and fiddly. Only a few days ago, he snuck in here disguised as a plumber and fixed my toilet so that it gushed when it should have flushed. It gave me quite a shock, I can tell you.'

'Yuk!' said the twins.

'But I still pretended it wasn't him,' continued Chad. 'I simply told myself it's one of the escaped murderers who frequent these parts. That's why I was so spooked when I picked up my viddy phone just now. He's left me a message!'

'What did it say, Chad? What did it say?' gasped the kids.

'It said…'

'Just a moment!' whispered Hugo, suddenly

holding up his hand for quiet. 'I thought I heard a noise coming from your food-processing area.'

'I do beg your pardon,' said Chad, turning a deep shade of pink and putting his hands on his stomach. 'I had baked beans for lunch. They always have that effect on me. Especially when I'm feeling spooked.'

'No, I mean from your *kitchen*,' said Hugo.

'Yes, I heard it, too,' muttered Hailey, glancing anxiously towards the door.

'I didn't hear a thing,' said Chad. 'And I know I set the intruder alarm.'

'Don't you think you'd better check it out?' said Hugo. 'Just in case.'

'I think you're probably imagining things,' said Chad. 'But just to put your minds at rest I'll—'

Chad never did get to finish his sentence. At that moment, there was a flash of bright, cold steel that seemed to come from nowhere. It was followed by a sort of horrid half-scream, half-choke that escaped from Chad's throat.

Hailey and Hugo watched in horror as the famous author slid from his rocking chair and slumped onto the carpet, writhing in agony, his eyes bulging.

67

Moments later, their stomachs began to lurch as they caught sight of a sticky, crimson stain spreading across their hero's chest. Chad's steaming blood was spurting and splashing, warmly and wetly, all over his yak-wool waistcoat!

Chapter Eleven
The Big Fight

Chad opened one eye and looked up at the two pale young faces that were staring anxiously down at him.

'Er… sorry about that,' he murmured as he sat up and began examining the tip of his little finger. 'I seem to have stabbed myself with my miniature pirate's cutlass pencil sharpener. It just sort of slipped. I am a clumsy clot, aren't I? I never could stand the sight of my own blood.'

'Don't worry!' said Hailey.

'Well,' said Chad. 'At least it wasn't *him* who shed my blood.' Then he yawned and stretched, saying, 'I think I'm going to have to retire.'

The children's jaws dropped. 'Oh no, Chad! Don't do that!' they cried. 'Millions of kids will be heartbroken.'

'What… if I go *to bed*?' said Chad.

'Ah, *that* sort of retire,' said Hugo. 'You had us worried there for a moment.'

'Ha!' laughed Chad. 'Don't fret, there's no chance of me giving up my writing. My remarkable brain is full of far too many untold brilliant stories. But right now, I'm dead beat. I bet you kids could use some shut-eye, too.'

'Sure could,' agreed the twins. 'It's not that late, but we've had quite a day!'

'OK,' said Chad. 'I'll take you to your bedroom. You'll find everything you need in there: clean towels, ready meals, fizzy drinks, that sort of thing.'

'Chad…' said Hailey, as he led them up to their magnificent, twin-bed room. 'Do you think we really *are* going to die tonight?'

'Well,' said Chad, 'perhaps things aren't quite so bad as I led you to believe. In fact, I think I was probably exaggerating when I said all that stuff about us being murdered in our beds. You know what us writers are like. Sometimes our overactive imaginations get the better of us and we begin dreaming up all sorts of terrible possibilities. Our minds can be our worst enemies.'

'They certainly can!' laughed the twins.

'So things will probably be just fine,' said Chad. 'And, don't forget, this place of mine is protected by a state-of-the-art, infra-blue-with-a-hint-of-pink CCTV burglar alarm that is an exact replica of the one they used on the Apollo Moon Probe. So, on second thoughts, *yes*, we're all gonna be as safe as houses. And don't worry about Tamara, I just *know* she'll turn up sooner or later.'

'Well, that's a relief,' sighed the twins.

But their relief, unlike Galapagos tortoises, deep-sea tube worms and Arctic clams, would turn out to be very, *very* short-lived.

After helping themselves to a couple of ready meals and some fizzy drinks, the exhausted twins climbed into their beds and sank into a deep and dreamless sleep.

But it wasn't to last.

A few moments later, Hailey was woken by a sound coming from the bedroom door. She opened one eye and was instantly aware that the handle was being turned very, *very* slowly.

'Hugo,' she hissed. 'There's someone trying to get into our room!'

By the time Hugo had woken up, a huge figure was silhouetted in the bedroom doorway, snorting and grunting like an asthmatic rhinoceros. Despite the darkness, it was just possible to make out that in one hand it clutched a coil of rope and, in the other, a huge axe!

'I've come for you!' it snarled, in a voice which turned the twins' blood to ice. A voice which was both strange and alien, but somehow *oddly familiar*. 'I'm your worst nightm—' It hesitated, scratched its head, then said, 'Yes, that's it! I'm your worst *nightmare*. I'm the thing you dread more than anything in the world.'

Closing the bedroom door behind it, so they were now plunged into total darkness, the huge figure began to move towards the terrified children, making horrid groaning noises and dragging one foot behind it. As it came close, the twins became aware of its horrid smell, a mixture of stale muffins, rotting fish and mouldy cheese.

Hailey reached for her bedside light and flicked the switch. Nothing happened. They remained in total darkness. Then, in quick succession, she tried the intruder panic button, the digital alarm clock, the radio, the hairdryer, the automatic tea maker, the microwave and the widescreen TV. Nothing! And that could only mean one thing – the power supply had been cut. Well, either that, or Chad was in the habit of wasting his money on incredibly useless electrical appliances. And now he, whoever *he* was, was standing at the end of Hailey and Hugo's beds and talking to them in a manner that was very, very frightening!

'I may not be able to write real good like what he do,' he snarled. 'But at least I don't wear big lady's pants! And I can sure *think up* some horrible stuff. Horrible stuff like I'm just about to do to you!' Then he began laughing insanely. Laughing insanely in a manner which was somehow *oddly familiar*.

The monstrous man moved round to Hugo's bed and then thrust his face so close to Hugo's that their noses were almost touching.

Seizing the opportunity, Hailey leapt from her bed and ran for the door, screaming, 'CHAD! CHAD! HELP US! PLEASE HELP US! WE'RE BEING MENACED BY AN ENORMOUS MORON ARMED WITH AN AXE AND A ROPE! CHAD, PLEEEEASE HELP US!'

She almost made it. But, such was the size of the bedroom that the man was able to put himself between her and freedom before she reached the door. He began to chase her around the room and it looked like things were going to end in tears.

But then, from somewhere below, in a far-flung corner of the enormous house, there came an almighty crash, as if a wall were being demolished, or a door wrenched from its hinges. It was immediately followed by a distant cry of 'Hang on in there, kids! I'm coming! I'm coming!' and the sound of feet pounding along corridors, up stairs, along more corridors, down stairs, up stairs, along yet more corridors, then up even *more* stairs and along even *more* corridors!

After what felt like ages, the bedroom door finally burst open and in charged a huge and heroic figure, who immediately hurled himself upon the intruder. The two men now began to struggle ferociously, groaning and moaning, gasping and cursing.

'Hurrah!' yelled Hailey. 'It's Chad come to rescue us from Sherwood U. Harm! Well, at least I *think* it is!'

The two huge figures crashed to the floor, spitting, snarling and gnashing their teeth like two wild beasts as they rolled around. They crashed out of the bedroom and into the corridor, where they struggled and grunted again, before rolling along its entire length, still spitting, growling and scratching, before tumbling THUMP! THUMP! THUMP! THUMPETY! THUMP! down two flights of stairs and over a balcony, never once ceasing their mighty struggle.

The twins charged after them, yelling encouragement to Chad. By the light of the moon it was now plain to see that, yes, it *was* he who had come to their rescue!

The next field of battle was Chad's sitting room. The struggling men positively smashed their way into it, sending sculptures, ornaments and paintings flying, all the time doing their best to overcome each other in the most horrid and painful ways possible.

From the sitting room they tumbled into Chad's Scribblarium, still biting, punching, gouging, scratching and kicking. And it was here, to the twins' *utmost* dismay, that they saw, *horror of horrors* that the monstrous stranger was finally getting the upper hand. In just minutes, he had Chad pinned to the floor. He gripped his shoulders in his huge fists and the great author's breath started to come in ever-weaker gasps.

It was plain to see that Chad was now completely at the mercy of Sherwood U. Harm.

The handsome writer's energy and strength were gushing from him like water from a bucket full of holes. It would only be a matter of moments before victory was the intruder's, then it would be the twins' turn to suffer. Without Chad, their fate appeared to be as good as sealed. They would both perish slowly and painfully at the hands of this monstrous maniac. And that would be that. Their great adventure would end in doom and disaster.

Well, it *would* have done, if it hadn't been for Hailey. Seizing the first object that came to hand, namely Chad's huge and heavy 'Golden Entrails' Award, she brought it crashing down on Sherwood U. Harm's head, knocking him senseless in an instant!

Chapter Twelve
Let's Play a Game

'Yeah! Way to go, sis!' cried Hugo. 'Now *I'm* going to bash him with a great big *computer*!'

But Hailey didn't allow her brother to do any such thing. Instead, she helped Chad to drag himself from under the motionless form of his attacker and get to his feet.

'Is it him?' gasped Hailey, still shocked by her own strength and violence.

Chad wiped his brow, picked up a torch and shone it on the unconscious figure, saying, 'It certainly is. Sherwood U. Harm himself. All six feet three inches of him. The no-talent loser. See, he's still all icy from hiding out in the woods. He must have been waiting for us to go to bed so he could break in and finish us off.'

It seemed to make sense. Despite the struggle, it was still possible to see that areas of Harm's clothes were coated in a thick layer of frost.

'But what about Tamara?' said Hailey. 'What can have happened to her?'

Chad frowned. 'There's no telling. We'll just have to hope she's OK. She's a big girl who knows how to take care of herself.'

'But, Chad, surely we should go and look for her?' urged Hailey. 'Now that Sherwood U. Harm's out of action, we have nothing to fear.'

'Don't be so sure,' said Chad. 'There's a good chance Harm's got accomplices out there, waiting for us to do just that. No, we must stay put. Then, come the morning, we'll put this joker in my pick-up truck, haul him off to the cops and organise a search for Tamara.'

'But she could be lying somewhere injured or dying from frostbite…' pleaded Hailey.

Chad held up his hand for silence. 'I've just said it's too risky. Don't you understand plain English? What we do is *stay put*. Goddit?'

Hailey nodded, deeply hurt by Chad's stern words and his failure to thank her for saving his life.

So stay put they did. The three of them sat, simply twiddling their thumbs and staring gloomily at the unconscious Sherwood U. Harm, who Chad had now securely trussed up, having discovered a pile of used trusses in his underwear drawer. As for sleep, all of them were far too wired by the excitement of the night for that. And there was now also a horrid tension in the air that hadn't been there before. A tension which the twins, especially Hailey, found most uncomfortable and disturbing. But then she remembered something she'd been planning ever since she and Hugo had won the 'Meet Chad Piranha' competition. Something that might just lighten things up a bit!

'I know,' she said cheerily. 'To pass the time until morning, let's play a game! What we do is this – one of us quotes a passage from one of your books, Chad. Then another of us has to carry it on.'

Before Chad could answer, she said, 'OK, we'll start with the first page of *Melvin's Arm*. "*It was early morning in the en-suite conversation pit of Beelzebub Cottage…*" What comes next, Chad?'

'Er, it escapes my memory right now,' mumbled Chad, suddenly looking very ill at ease, if not to say completely panic-stricken. 'And anyway, I don't want to play this stupid game!'

'"*Professor Lynette Cumberpatch and her husband, Doctor Dwayne Cumberpatch, the world famous experts on the weird and unexplained, were just in the middle of a particularly stimulating argument about the paranormal*".'

'Wow, Chad!' gasped Hugo. 'That was word perfect, and you said it all without moving your lips.'

But Hailey knew otherwise. It wasn't Chad who'd finished the quote so brilliantly. It was Sherwood U. Harm. He was now conscious and staring up at them.

'Would you like me to go on?' he said, in a voice as warm and reassuring as freshly baked apple pie and custard.

'Take no notice of him,' snapped Chad, his own voice now decidedly harsh and filled with menace. 'He only knew that because he's read my books.'

'Or maybe it's because I *wrote* your books,' responded Sherwood, quick as a flash. 'And maybe that's because *I* am the *real* Chad Piranha. And you, Sherwood U. Harm, are *pretending* to be me!'

'Shut it, before I clock you one,' snapped Chad, rising to his feet and snatching a roll of sticky tape from the desk, obviously intending to seal Sherwood's lips with it.

However, before he could do so, Hugo, still slightly behind with the plot, cried, 'This quoting game is great fun, isn't it? My turn now. I'll do the *Melvin's Arm* bit where the girls take his photo at the swimming pool.'

And that was it! In an instant, a light bulb the size of a hot-air balloon went on in Hailey's brain, and she finally put her finger on the thought that had been niggling away at her ever since they'd posed with the 'Golden Entrails'

Award. *Photographs*! Chad had let them take his photo over and over again in the Scribbularium. And Chad Piranha never let *anyone* take his photo.

'You aren't Chad Piranha, are you?' she said calmly.

Chapter Thirteen
Sherwood

'Got it in one, kid!' said Sherwood U. Harm, as he reached beneath Chad's desk and produced a very scary-looking gun, which he then proceeded to point at the twins. 'Had you fooled with my super-cool acting though, didn't I? You can thank the Wisconsin School of Corrective Drama Therapy for that!'

'So it was *you* who came into our bedroom and scared the life out of us!'

'Exactly! And if it hadn't been for *him* barging in when he did, I'd have finished you both off,' said Sherwood, nodding at the real Chad. 'So me and Chaddy-boy here could get back to work on turning *me* into a top-class author.'

'Which, I can assure you, was *not* a voluntary arrangement,' said the real Chad. 'This joker ambushed me three days ago. Cold-cocked me with his gun then dragged me to my Scribbularium and threatened to blow out my brains if I didn't tell him where I get all my ideas from.'

'But then we switched on his PC and I saw that email from Dead Good Books,' said Sherwood. 'The one saying how you pair of pains-in-the-pants and that pesky editor of his would be arriving any time soon. So I put him *on ice* while I went out and blocked the road with the big tree.'

'So it *wasn't* beavers!' gasped Hugo.

'Well, if I'm honest, they did help a *bit*,' said Sherwood. 'But I did all the really difficult stuff.'

'So *that's* why you didn't want us to look inside the walk-in freezer!' exclaimed Hailey. Then turning to the real Chad, she said, 'And here's me thinking you were all icy because you'd been hiding out in the woods. You poor thing, you've been locked in there all the time.'

'Yes, I have,' said Chad. 'But I knew you kids were coming and realised that the only way I could stop anything terrible happening to you was to stay warm and alert. So for the past two days I've been jogging round and round the freezer, keeping myself alive by eating frozen-yoghurt ice cream. When I heard your heartbreaking screams for help it sort of drove

85

me berserk, giving me the strength of ten men and enabling me to smash my way out of the freezer.'

'And *that's* when you came to rescue us,' said Hailey, blushing. 'And if I hadn't knocked you unconscious, *you* would have won the fight!'

Chad nodded, smiling ruefully.

'I'm really, really sorry,' said Hailey, now realising that she'd almost killed the most famous children's horror-fiction writer in the world.

'Don't worry, kid,' Sherwood laughed cruelly. 'You did me a big favour!'

'But what about Tamara?' piped up Hugo, now finally getting a handle on the unfolding situation. 'Where's Tamara?'

'You'll have to ask *him* that,' said Chad, casting a steely glance at Sherwood.

'Ha ha ha!' shrieked Sherwood, in that now oh-so-familiar *mad* laughter. 'You won't be seeing old rubber lips again. She really *did* have an encounter with a *noose*. Just after she left you to get help, I bushwhacked her, then tied her to a tree. She's probably still there now. Well, what's left of her. Now that the grizzly bears, wolves and mountain lions have had their fill.'

'Aren't you forgetting the guinea pigs?' said Hugo.

'All right, them, too!' Sherwood snapped irritably.

'And the beavers!' added Hailey.

'Actually, I think beavers are herbivores,' said Sherwood. Then he grinned cruelly and snarled, 'But *whatever*. The main thing is that tombstone teeth is worm food now!'

'That's what *you* think, sleazebag,' said a voice behind him. And everyone whirled around to see Tamara standing in the doorway. She was wearing her frosted-up sunglasses and holding a really big cucumber. 'Yes, I'm back, scumball,' she hissed. 'And I'm very, *very* angry!'

Then, with her lips curled back to expose her huge, white teeth, she took careful aim with the massive cucumber, pointing it directly at Sherwood's heart.

'But… but…' spluttered Sherwood, looking as if he truly believed Tamara was a ghost. 'I tied you up with every knot known to humankind and boy scouts. There was *no way* you could have survived out there in the wild!'

'And I wouldn't have done,' said Tamara, 'if it hadn't been for the stranger. Just as two huge grizzly bears and a couple of dozen guinea pigs were about to tear me to pieces, this really cool-looking guy comes charging out of the trees. Next minute, his fists were going like pistons, *blatt*! *blatt*! *blatt*! Those guinea pigs didn't stand a chance. Nor did the grizzlies. That guy gave those bears a whooping like I've never seed before!'

'Actually, Tamara, it's *seen* before,' said Chad.

'Sorry, Chad!' said Tamara. 'Anyway, this true hero unties me, gives me a peck on the cheek, yells "See you, babe! I got business to attend to" and goes dashing off into the woods!'

'What happened next?' asked the twins.

'I made my way here!' said Tamara. 'Then I used my personal key to get into the kitchen. Where I just happened to spot this big gun. How's that for luck!' She walked up to Sherwood and began jabbing his chest with the cucumber. 'So, you sleazebag, no-talent, arsonist creep! Who's gonna pull the trigger first? I'm ready when you are. OK, you might blow me away, too. But, so *what*! It'll be worth it just to see the expression on your face when I blast your guts out.'

'Tamara, it's a cucumber!' said Hailey

'What's a cucumber?' said Tamara.

'Your gun!' said Hugo.

'Is it?' cried Tamara. Then the end of her cucumber broke off and fell on the floor as she gave Sherwood an extra hard poke with it. 'Oh shucks!' she cried. 'I've gone and done it again, haven't I? I really must go to the opticians and get myself some contract lenses.'

'Don't kid yourself,' snarled Sherwood U. Harm. 'You ain't gonna be going to no optician. Or anywhere else for that matter. Get over there with the rest of them. It's time for all you guys to go to the great big bookshop in the sky!'

Then, once Tamara had joined the twins and Chad, Sherwood U. Harm put the gun against Hailey's head and said, 'I think we'll start with you.'

Chapter Fourteen
Hairy Ears

Sherwood took a deep breath, smiled his evil killer's smile, laughed his maniac's laugh and snarled, 'This is it then, kid. Say goodbye to your buddies.'

Hailey went numb from head to toe and her eyes grew wide with terror as she felt the cold steel of the gun pressing into the tender skin of her temple.

Then, just as Sherwood U. Harm flicked off the gun's safety catch, there was an enormous *crash*! and the big window of Chad's Scribbularium exploded into a thousand pieces. In the next instant, a small but remarkably tough-looking, corduroy-clad figure hurled itself at Sherwood, knocking him away from Hailey.

Next there were three ear-shattering *bangs*!, as Sherwood loosed off three wild shots. Three wild shots that destroyed Chad's PC and his complete store of back-up discs, but mercifully left Hailey unharmed.

Now Dwayne Dobson's right fist socked into Sherwood's jaw, while his left fist gave Sherwood a shattering blow to the side of his head. *Blatt! blatt! blatt!* You could almost see the stars whirling in front of his eyes. But then Sherwood seemed to steady himself. He brought the gun up again and pointed it straight at his attacker.

And that was the moment when Dwayne's absolutely lightning-fast right fist clattered into Sherwood's jaw yet again, lifting him off his feet and depositing him on the opposite side of the Scribbularium.

Dwayne was on him in a flash, pummeling him almost senseless with a series of devasting slaps, punches and pinches. Before Sherwood knew what was happening, Dwayne was wrapping coil after coil of rope around him – the very same rope that Sherwood had been carrying when he came to 'rescue' the twins in the forest.

'Wow!' cried Tamara. 'It's my little hero… *again*! I thought he sorted those grizzlies real good. But that was *awesome*!'

'Think nothing of it, babe!' said Dwayne, stuffing the rope's free end up Sherwood's left nostril.

'Dwayne!' gasped Hailey. 'How did *you* get here?'

'It's a long story,' said Dwayne, who somehow appeared taller, more athletic and definitely loads better-looking than he had when the twins last saw him.

'But to be brief,' he said, in a voice that was most certainly deeper and much, much more reassuring than they'd ever heard him sound before, 'as you know, I was real miffed about losing the writing competition. So, in a way which I now realise was childish, impetuous and foolish, to say the least, I decided to follow you up here.

'Well, things didn't go according to plan. For starters, 20 minutes after your plane landed, I was discovered hiding in the cargo hold, so I had to make a pretty fast getaway. What with the dogs and rocket-propelled grenades, it was a close-run thing, but I finally managed to give airport security the slip.

'After that, I hitched a lift on the Ratskill County interstate highway. As luck would have it, I was picked up by a gang of human-organ traders who wanted my kidneys, lungs, heart, spleen and other bits in exchange for the ride. A real bunch of misfits and losers if ever I saw one. But, using a mixture of raw courage and youthful energy, it didn't take me long to see *them* off! Then, "borrowing" their truckload of frozen appendixes, I motored up into the Ratskills, only to have the truck break down. And what should happen when I'm trying to fix it, but this dirty great mountain lion jumps me and tries to take a bite out of my backside. So I had to deal with *that*. Phew, what a scrap!

And hardly had I recovered when I was attacked by a pack of vicious wolves. Talk about getting into some wuff stuff!'

Dwayne paused, and a devil-may-care grin creased his newly handsome features. He wiped a bead of sweat from his forehead and said, 'It really did seem like one thing after another. But you know what, guys, having bad stuff happen to you sometimes has the effect of making you a better person, a fitter person, and a less mixed-up sort of person. And that's what's happened to me, I guess. During the last couple of months, my actual body's also been going through some very weird and dramatic changes, too! You know, like getting, much, *much* more muscley! And hairs are sprouting in the weirdest places, like in my ears. I mean, how crazy is *that*?'

'Publicity!' said Tamara. 'You call it publicity when that happens.'

'Actually Tamara, I think you might mean *puberty*,' said Chad.

'But I thought that just meant that you're old enough to go into pubs!' said Sherwood.

'Be quiet!' said Hugo. '*You've* said quite enough for one day. Go on, Dwayne, we're all hairy ears.'

'Well,' said Dwayne, 'what I suppose I'm *trying* to say is that these recent experiences have turned me into an all-new, much-improved Dwayne Dobson. And Hailey, if I'm honest, what was behind my crazy desire to chase you up here to the Ratskills in the first place is the deep love I've been feeling for you for some time now. So, I hope you don't mind if I put my arm around you, and say, "Hailey, will you be my girlfriend?"'

'Actually, I'm Hugo!' said Hugo, gently removing Dwayne's arm from around his shoulder. 'That's Hailey over there!'

And that's about it! The twins and Dwayne finally got to spend a few fabulous days at Macabre Manor with the real Chad Piranha and the dazzling Tamara Tippex-Tripewrangler. Sherwood U. Harm got put away for a long, long time and the all-new Dwayne Dobson became Hailey's boyfriend.

The only thing which did cause some all-round upset was the fact that Sherwood's three wild shots not only destroyed Chad's PC, but his new work-in-progress and all the back-up copies, too! For a few brief and painful moments everyone was pretty devastated by this discovery, until Hailey said, 'Don't worry, Chad, now you've got a brilliant *new* story to write. In other words, everything that's taken place over the last few days.'

'Yes,' said Hugo. 'And you could call it *Dying To Meet You*.'